Happy Birthday
Love to Nicole

Sydney, Keith
Kylie & Howard
May 1995

For Lonika

VIKING
Published by the Penguin Group
Viking Penguin, a division of Penguin Books USA Inc.,
375 Hudson Street, New York, New York 10014, U.S.A.
Penguin Books Australia Ltd, Ringwood, Victoria, Australia
Penguin Books Canada Ltd, 2801 John Street, Markham, Ontario, Canada L3R 1B4
Penguin Books (N.Z.) Ltd, 182-190 Wairau Road, Auckland 10, New Zealand

First published in Great Britain by ABC, 1990
First American edition published in 1991

1   3   5   7   9   10   8   6   4   2

Copyright © Lucy Dickens, 1990

All rights reserved

Library of Congress catalog number: 90-50128
ISBN 0-670-83577-3

Printed and bound in Great Britain
by MacLehose & Partners for Imago

Rosy's Pool

by Lucy Dickens

VIKING

Rosy's mother came home from the store.
"Look in the bag, Rosy," she said.

Rosy peeked inside.

There was something red and green and shiny. Rosy pulled it out.

"It's a wading pool!" said Sam. "Let's blow it up."
"Rosy do it," said Rosy.
Rosy blew. Sam blew. Their mother blew. Finally the pool was ready.

"Let's take it out," said Sam.
"Rosy do it," said Rosy.

"Let's fill it," suggested Sam.
"Rosy do it," said Rosy.
Sam filled bucket after bucket and
Rosy emptied them. Their friends,
the twins, watched.

"Let's try it," said Sam.
"Rosy do it," said Rosy. She put on
her favorite swimsuit and tested
the water with her toe.
"Cold," said Rosy.

"Can we play in your pool?" called the twins.

Rosy and the twins squeezed into the pool.

Sam played with the hose.

"Who wants supper?"
called their mother.
"Rosy," said Rosy.
As soon as they were
in the kitchen, the dogs
jumped into the pool.
"They're swimming,
too!" said Sam.

"Oh, no!" said their mother, as the dogs came in and shook water all over the kitchen. Rosy just clapped her hands.

"Time for bed," said Rosy's mother.

Rosy peeked out the window.

"Bird," said Rosy.

"Everyone wants to play in your pool, Rosy," said her mother.

"But now it's time
for bed."